Anansi and Mr Snake

and other stories

Miles
KeLLY

First published in 2011 by Miles Kelly Publishing Ltd
Harding's Barn, Bardfield End Green, Thaxted, Essex, CM6 3PX, UK

2 4 6 8 10 9 7 5 3 1

Publishing Director Belinda Gallagher
Creative Director Jo Cowan
Editor Amanda Askew
Senior Designer Joe Jones
Production Manager Elizabeth Collins
Reprographics Anthony Cambray, Stephan Davis, Lorraine King, Jennifer Hunt

ISBN 978-1-84810-495-2

Printed in China

British Library Cataloguing-in-Publication Data
A catalogue record for this book is available from the British Library

ACKNOWLEDGEMENTS
Artworks are from the Miles Kelly Artwork Bank

Cover artwork by Frank Endersby (Beehive Illustration)

Every effort has been made to acknowledge the source and copyright holder of each picture.
Miles Kelly Publishing apologises for any unintentional errors or omissions.

Made with paper from a sustainable forest

www.mileskelly.net
info@mileskelly.net
www.factsforprojects.com

Contents

The Swineherd

By Hans Christian Andersen

THERE WAS ONCE a poor prince. He possessed a kingdom which, though small, was large enough for him to marry on, and married he wished to be.

Now it was certainly a little bold of him to say to the emperor's daughter, "Will you marry me?" but he did, for his name was known far and wide. There were hundreds of princesses who would gladly have said yes, but would she say the same?

Well, we shall see.

On the grave of the prince's father grew a rose tree, a very beautiful rose tree. It only bloomed every five years, and then bore but a single rose, but oh, such a rose! Its scent was so sweet that when you smelt it you forgot all your cares and troubles. And he had also a nightingale that could sing as if all the beautiful melodies in the world were shut up in its little throat. This rose and this nightingale the princess was to have, and so they were both put into silver caskets and sent to her.

The emperor had them brought to him in the great hall, where the princess was playing 'Here comes a duke a-riding' with her ladies-in-waiting. And when she caught sight of the big caskets that contained the presents, she clapped her hands for joy.

"If only it were a little pussycat!" she said. But the rose tree with the beautiful rose came out.

"But how prettily it is made!" said all the ladies-in-waiting.

"It is more than pretty," said the emperor.

But the princess felt it, and then she almost began to cry.

"Ugh! Papa," she said, "it is not artificial, it is real!"

"Ugh!" said all the ladies-in-waiting, "It is real!"

"Let us see first what is in the other casket before we begin to be angry," said the emperor, and out came

the nightingale. It sang so
beautifully that one could
scarcely utter a cross word
against it.

"Superbe! Charmant!"
said the ladies-in-waiting,
for they all chattered French,
each one worse than the other.

"How much the bird reminds me of the musical
snuff box of the late empress!" said an old courtier.
"Ah, yes, it is the same tone, the same execution!"

"Yes," said the emperor, and then he wept like a
little child.

"I hope that this, at least, is not real?" asked the
princess.

"Yes, it is a real bird," said those who had brought it.

"Then let the bird fly away," said the princess, and
with that, she would not allow the prince to come.

But he was not put off. He painted his face brown
and black, drew his cap well over his face, and knocked
at the door. "Good day, emperor," he said. "Can I get a
place here as servant in the castle?"

"Yes," said the emperor, "but there are so many who
ask for a place that I don't know whether there will be
one for you, but, still, I will think of you. Actually, it

has just occurred to me that I want someone to look after the swine, for I have so very many of them."

And the prince got the job of imperial swineherd. He had a wretched little room close to the pigsties. Here he had to stay, but the whole day he sat working, and when evening came he had made a pretty little pot. All round it were little bells, and when the pot boiled they jingled most beautifully and played the tune:

"Where is Augustus dear? Alas!

 He's not here, here, here!"

But the most wonderful thing was, that when one held one's finger in the steam of the pot, then at once one could smell what dinner was ready in any fireplace in the town. That was indeed something quite different from the rose.

Now the princess came walking past with all her ladies-in-waiting, and when she heard the tune she stood still and her face beamed with joy, for she also could play 'Where is Augustus dear?'

It was the only tune she knew, but that she could play with one finger.

"Why, that is what I play!" she said. "He must be a most accomplished swineherd! Listen! Go down and ask him what the instrument costs."

And one of the ladies-in-waiting had to go down,

but she put on wooden clogs because of the mud. "What will you take for the pot?" asked the lady-in-waiting.

"I will have ten kisses from the princess," said the swineherd.

"Oh my, heaven forbid!" said the lady-in-waiting.

"Yes, I will sell it for nothing less," replied the swineherd.

"What did he say?" asked the princess urgently, when the lady-in-waiting returned.

"I really hardly like to tell you," answered the lady-in-waiting.

"He is disobliging!" said the princess. But she had only gone a few steps when the bells rang out so prettily:

"Where is Augustus dear?

Alas! he's not here, here, here."

"Listen!" said the princess. "Ask him whether he will take ten kisses from my ladies-in-waiting."

"No, thank you," said the swineherd. "Ten kisses from the princess, or else I keep my pot."

"That is very tiresome!" said the princess. "But you must put yourselves in front of me, so no one can see."

And the ladies-in-waiting placed themselves in front of the princess and then spread out their dresses, so the swineherd got his ten kisses, and she got the pot.

What happiness that was! The whole night and the whole day the pot was made to boil. There was not a fireplace in the whole town where they did not know what was being cooked, whether it was at the chancellor's or at the shoemaker's.

The ladies-in-waiting danced and clapped their hands.

"We know who is going to have soup and pancakes – isn't it interesting?"

"Yes, very interesting!" said the first lady-in-waiting.

"But don't say anything about it, for I am the emperor's daughter."

"Oh, no, of course we won't!" said everyone.

The swineherd – that is to say, the prince (though they did not know) – let no day pass without making something, and one day he made a rattle which, when it was turned round, played all the waltzes and polkas that had ever been known since the world began.

"But that is superbe!" said the princess as she passed by. "I have never heard a more beautiful composition. Listen! Go down and ask him what this instrument costs, but I won't kiss him again."

"He wants a hundred kisses from the princess," said the lady-in-waiting who had gone down to ask him.

"He is mad!" said the princess, and then she went on, but she had only gone a few steps when she stopped.

"One ought to encourage art," she said. "I am the emperor's daughter! Tell him he shall have, as before, ten kisses, the rest he can take from my ladies-in-waiting."

"But we don't at all like being kissed by him," said the ladies-in-waiting.

"That's nonsense," said the princess, "and if I can kiss him, you can, too."

So the ladies-in-waiting had to go down to him again.

"A hundred kisses from the princess," said he, "or each keeps his own."

"Put yourselves in front of

us," she said then, and so all the ladies-in-waiting put themselves in front, and he began to kiss the princess.

"What can that commotion be by the pigsties?" asked the emperor, who was standing on the balcony. He rubbed his eyes and put on his spectacles. "Why those are the ladies-in-waiting playing their games, I must go down to them." What a hurry he was in!

As soon as he came into the yard he walked very softly, and the ladies-in-waiting were so busy counting the kisses and seeing fair play that they never noticed the emperor. He stood on tiptoe.

"What is that?" he said, when he saw the kissing, and then he threw one of his slippers at their heads just as the swineherd was taking his eighty-sixth kiss.

"Be off with you!" said the emperor, for he was very angry. And the princess and the swineherd were driven out of the empire.

Then the princess stood still and wept, the swineherd was scolding, and the rain was streaming down.

"Alas, what an unhappy creature I am!" sobbed the princess. "If only I had taken the beautiful prince! Alas, how unfortunate I am!"

And the swineherd went behind a tree, washed the black and brown off his face, threw away his old clothes, and then stepped forward in his splendid dress, looking so beautiful that the princess was obliged to curtsey.

"I now come to this. I despise you!" he said. "You would have nothing to do with a noble prince, you did not understand the rose or the nightingale, but you would kiss the swineherd for the sake of a toy. This is what you get for it!" And he went into his kingdom and shut the door in her face, and she had to stay outside singing:

"Where's my Augustus dear?
Alas! he's not here, here, here!"

Master and Man

By T Crofton Croker

BILLY MAC DANIEL was once as likely a young man as ever emptied a glass, or handled a club. Fearing and caring for nothing, Billy Mac Daniel fell into bad company, for surely the fairies (also known as the good people) are the worst of all company anyone could come across.

It so happened that Billy was going home one frosty night not long after Christmas. The moon was round and bright, and he felt pinched with cold.

"By my word," chattered Billy, "a drop of good liquor would be no bad thing to keep a man's soul from freezing in him, and I wish I had a full measure of the best."

"Never wish it twice, Billy," said a little man in a three-cornered hat, bound with gold lace, and with great silver buckles on his shoes, and he held out a glass as big as himself, filled with good liquor.

"Success, my little fellow," said Billy Mac Daniel, unafraid, though he knew the little man belonged to 'the good people'. "Here's to your health, anyway, and thank you kindly, no matter who pays for the drink," and he took the glass and drained it to the very bottom without ever taking a second breath.

"Success," said the little man, "and you're heartily welcome, Billy, but don't think to cheat me as you have done others – out with your purse and pay me."

"I am to pay you?" said Billy, "Could I not just take you up and put you in my pocket?"

"Billy Mac Daniel," said the little man, getting very angry, "you shall be my servant for seven years and a day, and that is the way I will be paid, so get ready to follow me."

When Billy heard this, he was sorry for having used such bold words towards the little man, and he felt that he had to follow the little man all night across the country, without any rest.

As the sun began to rise, the little man turned round to Billy and said, "You may now go home, Billy, but don't fail to meet me in the fort-field tonight, or it may be the worse for you in the long run. If I find you a good servant, you will find me a good master."

Home went Billy Mac Daniel, and though he was tired and weary, he could not get a wink of sleep for thinking about the little man. He was afraid not to do his bidding, so up he got in the evening, and went to the fort-field. He was not long there before the little man came towards him and said, "Billy, I want us to go on a long journey tonight, so saddle two horses."

"If I may be so bold, sir," said Billy, "I would ask which is the way to your stable, for not a thing do I see except the old thorn tree in the corner of the field, and the stream running at the bottom of the hill."

"Go over to that bit of a bog, and bring me two of the strongest rushes you can find," said the little man.

Billy did so, wondering what the little man would do, and he picked two of the stoutest rushes he could find, and brought them back to his master.

"Get up, Billy," said the little man, taking one of the rushes from him and striding across it.

"Where?" said Billy.

"Why, upon horseback, like me," said the little man.

"Are you after making a fool of me," said Billy, "bidding me get on horseback upon that bit of rush?"

"Up! Up! And no words," said the little man, looking very angry. So Billy, thinking all this was in joke, straddled the rush.

"Borram! Borram! Borram!" cried the little man three times (which, in English, means 'become big'), and Billy did the same after him. Suddenly the rushes swelled up into fine horses, and away they went at full speed. Billy had put the rush between his legs, without much minding how he did it, so he found himself sitting on horseback the wrong way. It was rather awkward, with his face to the horse's tail, and so quickly had his steed started off with him that he had no power to turn round. There was nothing for it but to hold on by the tail.

At last they came to their journey's end, and stopped at the gate of a fine house. "Now, Billy," said the little man, "do as you see me do, and follow me close."

The little man then said some queer kind of words, out of which Billy didn't understand, but repeated.

In they both went through the keyhole of the door, and through one keyhole after another, until they got into the wine cellar, full of all kinds of wine.

The little man fell to drinking as hard as he could, and Billy did the same. "The best of masters are you surely," said Billy to him.

"I have made no bargain with you," said the little man, "and will make none, but up and follow me." Away they went, through keyhole after keyhole. They mounted the rushes at the hall door, and scampered off, kicking the clouds before them like snowballs, as soon as the words, 'Borram, Borram, Borram', had passed their lips.

When they came back to the fort-field, the little man dismissed Billy, bidding him to be there the next night at the same hour. Thus did they go on, night after night, shaping their course one night here, and another night there, sometimes north, sometimes east, and sometimes south, until there was not a gentleman's wine cellar in all Ireland they had not visited.

One night Billy's master said to him, "Billy, I shall want an extra horse tonight, for maybe we may bring back more company than we take." So Billy brought a third rush, much wondering who it might be that would travel back in their company.

Away they went, Billy leading the third horse, and never stopped until they came to a snug farmer's house, in the county Limerick. Within the house there was a great deal of noise and the little man stopped outside. Then turning round all of a sudden, said, "Billy, I will be a thousand years old tomorrow!"

"God bless us, sir," said Billy, "will you?"

"Don't say those words again, Billy, as you will be my ruin forever. I have come all this way because I think it is time for me to get married. And in this house is young Darby Riley who is going to be married to Bridget Rooney. She is a tall and comely girl, and has come of decent people, I think of marrying her myself, and taking her off with me."

"And what will Darby Riley say to that?" said Billy.

"Silence!" said the little man, putting on a severe look. He began saying the queer words that had the power of passing him through the keyhole as free as air, and which Billy thought himself mighty clever to be able to say after him.

In they both went. For the better viewing the company, the little man perched on one of the big beams and Billy did the same.

There they were, both master and man, looking down upon the fun that was going forward, and under

them were the priest
and piper, the family of
Darby Riley, the family of Bridget
Rooney, and plenty to eat and drink on the
table for every one of them.

Now it happened, just as Mrs Rooney cut the pig's
head, that the bride gave a sneeze, which made
everyone at table start, but no one said 'God bless us'.
The bridal feast went on without the blessing.

"Ha!" exclaimed the little man, throwing one leg from under him with a joyous flourish, and his eye twinkled with a strange light. "I have half of her now, surely. Let her sneeze but twice more, and she is mine."

Again the fair Bridget sneezed, but it was so gently that few except the little man seemed to notice, and no one thought of saying 'God bless us'.

All this time, Billy could not help thinking what a terrible thing it was for a nice girl of nineteen to marry an ugly little man, who was a thousand years old.

At this moment, the bride gave a third sneeze, and Billy roared out with all his might, "God bless you!"

No sooner was it uttered than the little man, his face glowing with rage, shrieked out in the shrill voice, "I discharge you from my service, Billy Mac Daniel – take that for your wages," and gave poor Billy a most furious kick in the back, which sent his unfortunate servant sprawling upon his face and hands right in the middle of the dinner table.

If Billy was astonished, how much more so was every one of the company into which he was thrown. But when they heard his story, Father Cooney laid down his knife and fork, and married the young couple there and then!

Baba Yaga, the Bony-legged Witch

A Russian folk tale

THERE WAS ONCE a wicked woman who hated her stepdaughter so much that she pushed the little girl out of the house and told her to go and borrow a needle and thread from Baba Yaga, the bony-legged witch. The girl's father was at work, so she had no one to turn to and she was terrified. Baba Yaga, the bony-legged witch, lived in the middle of the deep, dark forest, in a hut that moved about on hens' legs. Nevertheless, the little girl dared not disobey her cruel stepmother, so off she went, alone and frightened.

The little girl was soon among tall, prickly trees that whispered all around her, and she quite forgot which way was which. Tears began to glisten in her eyes and

slowly roll down her flushed cheeks.

"Do not weep, little girl," came a cheerful voice. The little girl looked up to see that a nightingale was talking to her. "You are a kind-hearted girl and I will tell you what I can to help you. Along the path, you will come across some objects. Pick them up and make sure you use them wisely."

So the girl set off again. As she walked along, she saw a neatly folded handkerchief lying among the pine needles, and she put it in her pocket. A little further on, she spied some ribbons that were dangling from the branches. She took those and slipped them into her pocket, too. A few steps on, she spotted a little can of oil, laying among some rocks. She picked up the oil can and placed it with the other things. Next, she came across a large bone and a maple leaf sprinkled with some juicy morsels of meat – then her pocket was full.

It wasn't long before some big iron gates came into view up ahead, and beyond them was the hut of Baba Yaga running about on its hens' legs. The little girl shivered with fear. Suddenly, a howling wind rose up, sending the branches of the trees whipping fiercely around her head. "I'll never get near that horrible hut at this rate," the little girl sighed, ducking the boughs coming at her thick and fast. Then she remembered the things she had collected along the way. Pulling out the ribbons from her pocket, she tied them carefully onto the trees. As soon as she did, the wind dropped to a gentle breeze and the branches became still.

Then the little girl tried to push open the gates, but a dreadful creaking and groaning tore through the air. She took the oil can from her pocket and covered the hinges with oil. After that, the gate opened without a squeak, and the girl passed through.

All of a sudden, a drooling, snarling dog came running at her out of nowhere, barking ferociously. Quick as a flash, the girl threw the big, juicy bone to the dog. He forgot his attack immediately and lay down to gnaw at his unexpected treat.

Now the only obstacle left to face was the hut itself, scuttling about on its awful scaly legs. And there, standing in the shadows, was the ugliest woman the girl had ever seen – a thin, bony figure with dark, shining eyes and long, green hair. It had to be Baba Yaga, the bony-legged witch.

"Come in, my dear," grinned the witch, showing her sharp, iron teeth. "While I'm searching for that needle and thread you want, you can have a nice bath and do my spinning for me." Baba Yaga gripped the girl's arm with her clawlike fingers and pulled her into the house. "Run her a bath and be quick!" she screamed at her pale-faced maid, before whispering, "Make sure you scrub her well, all ready for eating." With a wry smile, Baba Yaga swept from the room, leaving them alone.

The pale-faced maid began to bustle about, filling the bath with water, and fetching soap and a hard, dirty scrubbing brush. The little girl saw that she was trembling with fear. "I am sorry that you have to live and work here," the little girl said. "Here, have this handkerchief as a little present to cheer you up."

"Oh, thank you," the maid sighed, gazing in delight at beautiful silky red handkerchief. "I will use a teacup instead of a jug to fill the bath, so you have more time to escape."

Then the little girl noticed a skinny black cat cowering in the corner. "You don't look as if you've eaten properly for ages," she said, stroking his tatty fur. "Here, have these scraps of meat."

"Oh, thank you," the skinny black cat purred, washing his paws. "I will do the spinning for you, so you have more time to escape. Now take this magic towel and comb, and run for your life. When you hear Baba Yaga coming, throw each of them behind you, one by one. Be quick and go right away."

So the girl took the magic towel and comb, and ran as quickly as she could into the shadows of the towering trees. Back at the hut, the cat sat at the spinning wheel, tangled the wool into a ball to hide behind, and began to spin.

Several times, the witch passed the open door of the room and peered in. But when she heard the whirr of the spinning wheel and saw the pile of tangled wool, she went away, content. But by and by, the witch began to get suspicious that the pile of wool wasn't getting smaller. "Are you sure you know how to spin properly?" she screeched.

"Yes," yowled the cat, trying to sound like the girl but failing.

Baba Yaga realized she had been tricked. She screamed with fury, her face turning scarlet. Rushing into the room, she grabbed the cat by the scruff of the neck. "Why did you let the girl escape?" she howled.

"You've never given me anything but leftovers," the cat hissed. "That kind girl gave me tasty morsels of meat."

Furious, Baba Yaga stalked over to the pale-faced maid and slapped her. "Why did you let the girl escape?" she growled.

"You've never given me a single present," the pale-faced maid shouted. "That kind girl gave me a lovely hanky."

Storming outside, Baba Yaga kicked the dog who was happily chomping on his bone. "Why did you let the girl escape?"

"You've never given me a bone or a treat," the dog barked. "That kind girl gave me a big, juicy bone to chew on."

With incredible force, Baba Yaga kicked the iron gates. "Why did you let the girl escape?" she shouted.

"You let us get all stiff and rusty," they creaked. "That kind girl soothed our aching joints with lashings of lovely oil."

Finally, Baba Yaga threatened the birch trees with an axe. "Why did you let the girl escape?" she howled.

"You've never once decorated our branches," they roared, "but that kind girl dressed us with ribbons."

Gnashing her iron teeth wildly, she jumped on her broomstick and raced off through the deep, dark forest after the little girl. Hearing the swish of the air, the little girl knew the witch was coming and so threw down the magic towel. Suddenly, a wide rushing river appeared before Baba Yaga, soaking her broomstick so badly that it could no longer fly. Spitting and cursing, Baba Yaga had to leave her broomstick and slowly wade across the river. Once she was free of the water, she began to run after the little girl.

Hearing the pounding of Baba Yaga's footsteps, the little girl knew the witch was coming, and so threw down the magic comb. All of a sudden, a rainforest sprang up in front of Baba Yaga, so thick and tangled that Baba Yaga could do nothing to find her way through it. Squawking and screaming, she stormed back to her dreary hut, shouting all the way.

With her home in sight, the little girl heaved a sigh of relief, especially when standing at the door of her house was her beloved father. She rushed to tell him all about her stepmother's evil plot. Her father was horrified. He sent the wicked woman out of the house at once and drove her into the magic rainforest. From that day to this, she has never been seen again.

Whatever became of her, the little girl and her father lived happily on their own, and pleased with her genorosity and thoughtful nature, the nightingale came to visit every day.

The Giant's Wife

An Irish legend

IN THE DAYS when giants lived in the north of Ireland, Finn McCool was the biggest, strongest, most handsome of them all – or so he thought. With his bare hands, Finn could rip a pine tree out of the ground. He could leap across a river in one bound. He could split a boulder in half with one swish of his axe. Surely he was the greatest giant who ever lived.

Now Finn had heard that there were clans of giants living in Scotland who had competitions throwing tree trunks and carrying boulders. That sounded to him like great fun. So Finn decided to build a road right across the sea, so he could walk across to see these Scottish giants without getting his feet wet. Pulling on his big black workboots, he kissed his wife Oonagh goodbye, and promised, "I'll be back in about a week – ten days, tops." Then he strode off over the hills to the coast.

Finn began to work hard, ripping rocks from the mountains and throwing them into the sea until they piled up above the water and began to form a road. He was only three days into the job when a friend of his arrived at the seashore. "Finn, I don't mean to worry you, to be sure," his friend said, "but there's gossip about a strange giant who's on his way to your house to flatten you. Some say that he's leapt across the sea from Scotland without needing a boat or a bridge. People say that he keeps a thunderbolt in his pocket. I've heard, too, that he has a magic little finger with as much strength in it as ten men put together!"

"Pah!" cried Finn, "I don't believe a word of it!" But secretly, he began to feel a little uneasy.

"One thing's for sure," his friend continued, "the stranger knows that everyone thinks you're the biggest, strongest, most handsome giant in all of Ireland, and he doesn't like it one little bit. He's made up his mind to find you and mince you into pieces!"

"We'll see about that!" bellowed Finn. "I'm going home right now to sit and wait for this pipsqueak of a giant. If he dares to show his face at my front door, I'll stamp on him and squash him like an ant!" Although Finn sounded brave, he was really rather worried.

The minute Finn arrived home, he sat down glumly at the kitchen table and told Oonagh all about the stories of the strange giant.

"If it's true, he'll beat me into mashed potatoes!" Finn moaned.

"You men are always boasting about your muscles, but sometimes you should use your brains instead," Oonagh laughed. "Now do as I say and leave everything else to me."

Oonagh quickly found nine round, flat stones and put them on a plate with a round flat oatcake, which she cleverly marked with a thumbprint so she could see which one it was. Meanwhile, Finn built an enormous baby's cradle and put it by the fireside, just as Oonagh had told him. Just then, Finn and Oonagh felt the ground begin to shake underneath them and a dark shadow fell across the house.

"It's him! He's here!" panicked Finn, running to and fro. "What shall I do?"

"Calm down," urged Oonagh, handing her husband a bonnet and a nightdress. "Put these on and climb into the cradle!"

Finn was far too scared to argue, and soon he was dressed up like a baby and lying cuddled up in the crib. Oonagh shoved a huge bottle of milk into his mouth and went to answer the door.

"WHERE IS FINN MCCOOL?" roared the massive giant. He was the biggest giant Oonagh had ever seen – and the ugliest! "WHEN I FIND HIM, I'M GOING TO RIP HIM TO SHREDS!" the giant bellowed.

"I'm afraid you've missed my husband," Oonagh

smiled sweetly. "He's away at the coast, building a road across the sea to Scotland. He'll be finished by teatime. You can come and wait for him if you like."

The massive giant growled something under his breath that may or may not have been a thank you.

Oonagh beckoned him inside. "Well, you'd better come in and have something to eat. You'll need to get your strength up if you're going to fight Finn. I have to say, you look like a dwarf next to my husband!"

In the cradle, Finn's teeth began to chatter. What on earth was his wife annoying the giant like that for?

"Have an oatcake," Oonagh offered the stranger, putting one of the round, flat rocks on his plate.

The greedy giant crammed it into his mouth and took a huge bite. "OW!" he roared, spitting bits of broken teeth all over the table.

"Oh dear, didn't you like it?" Oonagh fussed. "They're the baby's favourite!" She gave Finn the oatcake with the thumbprint. He ate it happily.

The strange giant peered into the cradle. "That's Finn McCool's baby?" he asked, highly surprised. "He's a whopper of a lad, isn't he?"

"Yes," sighed Oonagh, tickling her husband under the chin while Finn cooed and gurgled as best he could. "He's got teeth already, you know. Here, put your finger into his mouth and feel. Go on."

Slowly, nervously, the giant put his little finger inside Finn's mouth.

CRUNCH! Finn bit down as hard as he possibly could – right through the bone!

"AAAAAAARRRRRRGGGGGGGGHHHHHHH!" roared the giant. "If Finn McCool's baby is that strong, I'm not hanging around to find out what Finn McCool is like!" And with that, he was out of the door and away before Finn could even leap out of the cradle.

Finn McCool never finished his road across the sea. If you go to Ireland today, you can still see it poking out into the water, half-finished. He wanted to rest with his beautiful, clever wife. So that's what he did!

Anansi and Mr Snake

A Caribbean folk tale

LONG, LONG AGO, deep in the luscious rainforests, animals and birds could talk and act very much like humans do. They spent their days working and playing together, and for most of the time, they lived in absolute harmony.

At the end of every day, all the creatures liked to gather to hear a bedtime story. As the sun dipped into the ocean, they would come out of the long, lush leaves of the dark, thick rainforest, and settle on the sandy shore. Every night, a different creature would sit at the head of the group and tell them a tale.

No one knew where the stories had come from, for none of them had ever been written down, but were passed on from generation to generation. Each creature told their story in their own style, leaving out parts that they didn't like, and adding in new ideas. And so the old stories were kept alive – made fresh and new, exciting and fun. The creatures never tired of telling or listening to the fanciful tales, night after night.

Storytelling time was known as Tiger time and all the stories were known as Tiger tales – because Tiger said so. Tiger was the strongest, most powerful animal – and so if Tiger wanted to use his name, they certainly didn't argue! Hardly anyone ever disagreed with Tiger. He made the creatures tremble and shake just by swinging his tail.

However, one particular evening, a small creature called Anansi dared to stand up to Tiger. Anansi was a spider who knew how to turn himself into a man… or maybe he was a man who knew how to turn himself into a spider. Whatever the case, he bravely stepped forwards out of the storytelling circle and spoke to Tiger.

"Mighty Mr Tiger…" Anansi began. But Tiger pretended not to notice him.

"Mighty and handsome Mr Tiger…" Anansi said, a little louder. But Tiger merely turned his head and sniffed.

"Mighty and handsome and intelligent Mr Tiger..." Anansi tried again, even louder this time. But Tiger just opened his jaws, yawned and looked away.

Now Anansi was really fed up – not just at Tiger's rudeness, but also because all the other creatures were smirking and sniggering.

"TIGER! ARE YOU DEAF?" Anansi shouted at the top of his voice.

In one bound, Tiger was nose to nose with Anansi. Anansi gulped, while all the other creatures shrank back nervously.

"Would you care to repeat that?" Tiger snarled.

"I said, excuse me, Mr Tiger, sir," Anansi squeaked.

"Hmmm," Tiger growled, settling down.

Anansi plucked up courage and continued. "Mr Tiger, sir – there are so many things named after you. I'd like something to be named after me, too."

All the creatures fell about laughing at Anansi's boldness. Even Tiger couldn't suppress a chuckle.

"What did you have in mind, little spider?" Tiger grinned.

"I'd like some tales to be called Anansi stories," Anansi announced.

Tiger was taken aback. He didn't want to share his stories with anyone. "Oh, I don't know about that," he

sniffed. "I'll have to think about it and let you know."
He paused for a moment, then said, "I've thought about
it – and the answer is… no."

But Anansi persisted. "Maybe I can pay you for some
stories?"

Tiger chuckled again. "Whatever could you offer me,
little spider, that I might want?" he said.

"I could bring you Mr Snake, all tied up, so you
could make him say sorry," Anansi said.

Now, everyone knew that Tiger and Snake had fallen
out. Neither could remember who had started the
argument, but each was refusing to talk until the other
one gave in and apologized.

Tiger thought carefully. He would love to see Snake
grovel – but how on earth would the little spider
manage it?

"Very well – it's a good trade," Tiger agreed. "You
have set yourself such a difficult task that if you can
achieve it, you deserve the stories."

With delight gleaming in his eyes, Anansi raced off
to the riverbank. He waited outside Snake's hole until
out of the darkness slithered Snake.

"May I have a word?" Anansi asked. "I've been telling
everyone that you're the longest creature, but they've
been laughing and saying that you're not."

"Have they, indeed?" bristled Snake, stretching out his coils. "Who do they think is longer?"

"Crocodile," Anansi fibbed. "But I thought if you measured yourself against a length of bamboo, I could then measure crocodile, and we could settle the argument. We both know that you're the longest!"

"That'sss true," hissed Snake. "Let'sss do it."

"Shall I tie you on?" Anansi suggested. "That way, we'll be sure to measure you when you're as stretched out as possible."

"Good idea," Snake agreed.

Anansi stretched and tied Snake to the bamboo. At last the job was done and he stepped back, gleefully.

"Congratulations! You're definitely longer than Crocodile," Anansi cheered. "But you're much more stupid!" And with that, he fetched Tiger.

Astonished, yet thrilled, Tiger kept his promise. From that day onwards, many tales were told about Anansi the spider – and they're called Anansi stories.